Songs of a Prairie Wildflower

Tenneil Mullin

Tellwell Talent
www.tellwell.ca

ISBN
978-0-2288-9430-8 (Paperback)

MERAKI

[may-rah-kee] Greek

(*n.*) To do something with soul, creativity, or love;
to put something of yourself into your work

THIS IS FOR *you*

This is for You
You who lays with me each night
Who sees the awe in a sunset
The miracle of the clouds
The delight of grazing deer
You who feels the pain of the Earth & its people
Whose heart swells with compassion
Who aches to see change
You who never stops loving me
Never ceases to understand
Forgive, accept, cherish

This is for You—it is always for You
You who is always by my side
Through tears & sorrow
Adventure, joy & laughter
You who craves a simple life
Surrounded by trees & wildflowers
With running water close by
You who seeks peace
The quiet of nature
The music of a birdsong
The dance of prairie grass

This is for You—all of it
To help you heal, shift & expand
To shine your light
For others to see & follow
To share your steadfast Hope
To step into your inherited power
To sprinkle your stardust
& make the world sparkle
With the wonder of magic
That is all around us, in us

This is for YOU

Songs
of a
Prairie
Wildflower

Repertoire

AWAKEN & EXPAND

HONOUR & CELEBRATE

REMEMBER & REFLECT

REST & RECOVER

TRIBUTE

Spring Recital

AWAKEN & EXPAND

ZENIPRISMA

I am a pristine bud
In an idyllic glade
Joyful & content
With who I am

A tightness begins to engulf me
Suffocating my creativity
I feel I must surrender
If I am to survive

It is a renewal
As I unfurl & reach
I am wild & tame
Grounded in my knowing

I flourish with warmth
I discover my inner awareness
Waiting to be rejuvenated
I awake in the spring sunshine

ZENIPRISMA—Buddhist & Taoist philosophy
[zen-ih-prism-uh] (n.) the heightened sense of inner
awareness experienced while basking in the Spring sun

EXHALATION

The melodious breeze
Grazes my flush cheeks
There is a renewed
Warmth in the air
Mother Earth
Is exhaling

After a season
Of rest
Her breath
Flows outward
With a hopeful
Uplifting anthem

The time has come
For a genesis
A fresh dawn
I rupture
Revived by
Her inspiration

IT'S HARD

Each day
Each step
I am fierce
I am resilient
But I'm drained
From having to be

I'm hopeful
Optimistic
But that too
Can be exhaustive
I can't show weakness
The threat of prey is real

But it is too hard
I feel depleted
From having to
Sustain the
Brave facade
For myself & others

I am caught in the claws
Of societal prey
I furl inward on the ground
Sinking into the pressure
That is piercing my once
Strong back

It is here
Pinned to the land
That my voice emerges
Raw & animalistic
I release anger & frustration
Back into the earth

Allowing the heartache
To overwhelm me
I spill salty tears
As I try to gain
Acceptance in
The unknown

This phase of
My life journey
Has a never-ending quality
The struggle is real
The questions linger
Stagnant around me

But my courage
Rears forth
An activation begins
I am being held up
I devour the sustenance
From within, from below

My rudimentary foundation
Emerges stronger
My soul is unscathed
I am primed
For the fated Hard
Once more

With faith & hope
I surrender to trust
That when another
Upheaval arises
I will be able
To liberate myself

Without fail
A new day will come
Deemed good or bad
It is merely another day
So I will embrace this
As the gift it is

One blessed day
The answers I seek
Will be laid before me
Preparing me
For the next challenge
I will grudgingly accept

This next Hard
Will hand me
The opportunity
To guide those who
Are stranded, alone
In their own turbid reality

I will lead the way
With my own light
As my luminous glow
Has been fuelled
In the trenches
Of the Hard

But for now,
IT'S just **HARD**

BREAKING THROUGH

The silence of my soul

Reaches up to the barren surface, gasping for life
I breath in the endless sea of depletion
My senses begin a slow awakening

I'm overcome with the incense of after
Of life once been
Rot, Dry, Loss

I notice the blue ribbon draped on high
Christened with cotton
Soft, Feathery, White

I devour blankets of divine wafers
Vanish & appear—again
Luscious, Fresh, Wet

My ears arouse to the brazen choir of flight
Sharing their journey songs
Music, Joy, Freedom

Arms outstretched I welcome the touch of golden waves
Beckoning me to call many a time
Eternal, Open, Warm

Shedding layers, shedding stories
I brave spring with promise anew
Life, Growth, Heart

I break through this intimate rhythm
Crying out from quenched hope
Renew, Wonder, Presence

FUNK

I float adrift
Not above
But below
In the depths
Of the darkness
My heaviness
Anchors me
To the obscurity where
My light cannot shine

Fear lurks
In the vast waters
Foreboding exudes
From the shadows
I am misplaced
Driven to submit
To bed down in
The murkiness of
Despair

I am doomed to
Bathe here for
A day
Or two
Or ten
Gathering courage
For the struggle
Back up
To the light

I've been
Here before
But each time
I become engulfed
I bring a little
More of myself
My expansiveness
With me
To help me rise

Will I ever
Anticipate
The downward spiral
Be armed & ready
Or will I be
Caught off guard
EVERY
DAMN
TIME

I thought
I learned
Thought I knew
How to keep
Myself aloft
It's chilling
Here in nadir
I don't feel
Myself

And yet
When I ultimately
& inevitably
Breach the surface
I clutch to me
A few more
Treasures
I've uncovered
In the underbelly

Over the course
Of my lifetime
My collection
Will be grand
It will tell
Tales of
Struggle
Discovery
& Resilience

RISE AGAIN

I'm struck again
Pushed down
Forced to remain insignificant
I dare to ask myself
Will I feel the sun once more?

The burden of rawness
Settles on me
Like a heavy cloak
A stinging slap to the face
Just as I had begun to rise

A delicate thought chooses me
Nudging me to remember
There was once Hope
Surging just below the surface
A slow, sure pulse

I hear Her tenderly calling
An alluring, familiar melody
After a deep, silent slumber
She extends me a guiding hand
Opportunity is offered

I hesitate, I've seen this afore
A flicker in the shadows
Beckoning me to stand tall
To reveal myself
To shine & share my light

What light? I ask
I've vanished into the dense fog
I've been kept here too long
Made small & dull
I'm empty, unable to dream

But She won't give up
She whispers to my soul
"Remember, remember
You are strong
You are enough"

I swallow the eternal calling
Welcoming it home within me
It breathes there, vibrating love
Barriers start to dismantle
One broken thought at a time

Shadows pursue refuge elsewhere
Light seeks, overflows & caresses
In caverns that have been dormant, forgotten
& I'm illuminated
Nourished with once-abandoned devotion

My essence ruptures forth
I am awakened
Hope is braved anew
I begin to rise with resolve & courage
No longer restrained or limited

My path transforms before me
I commence the quest for purity
Amidst a knowing in my soul
Great pain births great joy
I RISE

READY

She has been resting a long time
She accepts this essential repose
She relishes these moments of silence
She has laid down her armour of strength
Knowing she will need it once more
& when she does
She will be ready

Mother Earth cradles her in her arms
Strong & soft, a loving embrace
Mother welcomes her to lay her weary head
She presents herself wholly
They both hold compassion for the circle
She accepts this gift with a grateful heart
She is ready

With a loving tenderness she allows herself this solitude
A time to dream, reflect, to purely be
To receive courage & teachings from Mother
The enlightened messages envelope her
Guiding her to rediscover her power
So when the season inevitably comes
She will be ready

The shift is coming, her soul senses it
Her time of rest is approaching an end
Peace has been offered & collected
She feels her soul rejuvenated
She gathers up encouragement
Gifted by Mother & a belief in herself
They both know she is ready

The opportunity has come for her to shine
To fully uncover herself
To reveal her innate beauty
Her renewal is gradual
Not because she hesitates
Rather, she understands the necessity for poise
She is ready

As she seeks to break free from the earth
The growth is arduous
She hears a calling overhead
With Mother calmly by her side
She is birthed anew
The sun kisses her delicate, soft face
"READY," proclaims the crocus

life

One step at a time
Up the glorious mountain trail
Down, barefoot into the grass
Through the deep, dark tunnel of depression
Toward the world of your dreams
In the murky waters of life

One step at a time
Up the ladder of change
Down after a big adventure
Through the grey skies of loss
Toward empowering the mind, body & soul
In the changing seasons of life

One step at a time
Up to the clear skies of understanding
Down inside you, uncovering the layers
Through the healing of hurt & dis-ease
Toward compassion, forgiveness & acceptance
In this one precious life

IN TIME

First a few slivers of green
Moss softens
The mighty crocus emerges
Tender, purple & strong
Delicate bluebells sway in the breeze
Anemones, buttercups
Wild roses & bergamot
From spring to summer
Each has its moment to thrive

Then an interlude
A transformation of colour
Goldenrods & sunflowers
Fields of brome & wheatgrass
Sage, silver & humble
Recovery awaits the ridge

We too are nature, cyclical
Interchanging winks
Shining on stage
With all our brilliance
Bowing out
Heart full of applause
To dream, balance & restore
Connected & together
In the bosom of Mother

So unfurl your flower, Shine
When the season arises for you
& then, accept the peacefulness
While others take bloom
Together we will all flourish
Together we can each BE

INTO THE *light*

I step into the light, the truth of myself
It is new, yet familiar, real

My knowing will no longer remain dormant
A subtle recognition
Binds myself & Life
Distrust flares up
Rules, shoulds & ideology
That has kept me caged
But I no longer fit
As I swell with my Knowing
I begin to place the lies
Power, greed & darkness
Packaged as the way, as truth
Meant to keep us obedient & narrow
To follow the masses
The path has been formed before you
With blood, sweat & tears
The road has been paved to blindly follow
But I glimpse an unbeaten trail
Can I trust the pull from within?

I decide for Me, chosen by Me
I will let my light lead the way
I will trust myself, my Knowing
Above all else
Beyond the shoulds, the forced rightness
My Knowing cannot be unheard
What was once a soft musing
Is now all there is
It will not be ignored
The doubts become muffled
The Knowing heightened
I violate their beliefs for my own
I extend myself unapologetically
Scars & all, my battle wounds
Beauty is all I see

REIKI

I am opened up
Bright, billowing light
Pours forth from my chest
In shades of pink & purple
My soul is exposed
Raw & beautiful

My gaze turns up
The heavens are dancing
Brilliant yellows & greens
Fill the vastness
Swirling to the heartbeat
Of the glorious spirit

The artistry is mesmerising
Subtle, gentle movements
Waltz across the sky
Composing a joyful melody
The colours are vibrant
My voice is called upon

The offer is presented
I claim the invitation
To come home
To be amid the stars
To bathe in love & acceptance
To receive

The brilliance I emanate
Caresses the outlying rim
Like a canvas
Absorbing a fresh hue
My light complements the
Sweeping beauty

We drift collectively
An evolution of colour
Something magical is waking
The strokes are graceful
Brushing an ever-changing
Mural of awareness

Aurora has welcomed me
My eyes brim with emotion
I know, I remember
My unique, precious light
Adds to the beauty of the world
I choose to **shine**

ODE TO MY GARDEN

Welcome Home
A space has been created for you
You are invited to take root
To seek out what you need
To survive & thrive

Feel the sunshine fall upon you
Soak up the essence of the earth
Dance & rejoice with the rain
Let the air envelope your spirit
Feel the growth from within

May I learn from you
While I tend & sing & watch
With my hands & heart I make space
For your generous gifts of life
I will accept with a gracious soul

Summer Recital

HONOUR & CELEBRATE

SOLASTA

My light vibrates outward
Overflowing, reaching
Seeking to pollinate
Moving to a rhythm
Guided by my heartbeat
I celebrate my thriving
Lush & enchanting
Like a prairie wildflower
Basking in a sun-drenched meadow
I too feel this luminous glow
As I move closer to myself
I honour this brilliance
I AM THE LIGHT

SOLASTA—Scottish
[so-las-ta] (adj.) luminous, shining

JOURNEY

It is time to celebrate
How far I have come
Leaps & bounds
Baby steps
Stumbling
Tripping up
Falling back
The journey
Has not been direct
But there has always
Been choice along the way
No right or wrong
I put trust in myself
I will reach my destination
Only to find another
& another
AND
A N O T H E R
Life is a journey
The sweet final
Release of breath
The ultimate terminal
So cherish & celebrate
Each obstacle
Each miracle
Your legacy is
Being penned

HEAD HIGH

Hold your head up high
Tall & proud
Do not bow to others
Or make yourself small
Walk with purpose
Brimming with confidence
A grateful smile in place

You may think you need
To keep your head down
To see where you are going
But with your head down
You don't know what
Of life's wonders you
Are missing out on

Trust you will be guided
In the right direction

i am

i am Everything & Nothing
Always & Sometimes
i am Complete & Bare
Wise & Naive
i am Light & Dark
Soft & Strong
i am Proud & Humble
Peace & Angst
i am Free & Bound
Growth & Loss
i am Goddess & Pupil
Fierce & Tender
i am Refined & Wild
North & South
i am Love & Sorrow
Open & Sealed
i am Warrior & Philosopher
Mother & Child

with
Patience & Love
Compassion & Acceptance

I AM

PREDETERMINED

The bluebell stands elevated
Majestic & humble
Scattered forth on the prairie
Delicate, amethyst bonnet
Dancing, ringing in the
Peaceful, teasing breath of Mother Earth

Composing a melody from within
One to be made clear
By those still enough to reap
The whispers
The teachings
The ballad that communicates to us all

The Earth weighs upon us
With rich, colourful prose
Influencing a spark of memory
As we drink in the vision & vibration
We are encompassed with love
& stimulated with knowing

My eyes are drawn high
As the birds speak out
Frolicking amidst the heavens
Reminding us that
Freedom is to be had
By all of Earth's creatures

Great & small
Me, You
The birds above
The bluebells below
From the noble dragonfly
To the ambitious ant

We all belong
We are chosen to revive
Our modest origin
To bare forth our brilliance
Our unique offering
Mother encourages this discovery

Once united in harmony
We can be brilliant angels
Ushering forth our radiant light
Shepherding those in due course
Witnessing with acceptance
Savouring the legacies

The present, what is
From the vital sky flare
Warming our features
To the cooling breath of Mother,
To the soil, her voluptuous body
That gives & sustains life

Capture the twinkle of your essence
Give thanks to your bluebell
That which gives you pause
Charms your mindful eye & heart
That which makes your soul smile
Imprinting a desire to be worthy

Allow this to be your guiding spirit
Be openhearted to the teachings
The spark it kindles by its own nature
Illuminate your radiance
For collectively we foster existence
This is our arrangement

THE *dance*

I accept the hand being offered to me
> A nervous smile in place
> My body hums with anticipation
>> I am invited to the dance
>>> Led by my ancestors, I take my initial step

I stumble, falter, my head spins
> My heart beats faster, my palms sweat
> I am hesitant, unsure

Breathe

I become aware of the hushed tone
I close my eyes, I breathe
> In & out

My spirit unearths the silence
I connect with my nature
> Knowing the beat from within
>> Reliable & sound
> Offering me life, performing my inherent song

I bare myself, eager to harmonize
>> The journey is sure, I am in position

To inherit the teachings, the songs
> I rise with them
>> My being warms, my essence radiates

Collectively we twirl & sway in harmony
It's an intricate ceremony
Expressive, graceful, hypnotic
The melody is ancient & sacred
I flow alongside my lineage

I come into being
I remember
The movement is familiar
Encircled in the bosom, an aura of home
I acknowledge the lead, all those before me
With a deep bow of gratitude
My thanks
Within their presence, their eternal light
I bare myself & create my solo
I reveal my truth, the trueness of my tribe
Steadfast, courageous, my body is my narrative
Of the here & now
Of this one precious life
I will compose my own song
I dance with this revelation
In honour of myself

flow

Once upon a time ...
This is not your rags to riches saga
Rather, the contrary
I am called to pen my own fairy tale
Of a narrative bathed in
Heavy, warm blood
Fragrant with the scent of life

Fierce women unite
Sharing stories
Gathering wisdom
Commemorating our female lineage
Being cleansed of the dogma SHOULD
Allowing the knowing to
Bed down in our wombs

Revering the legacy formed within
Our delicate, soft folds
Celebrating our enchanting bodies
Alongside sister moon
It is not a burden
That we must bear
But rather an honour

Called to conceive a generation
Let us bloom in unison
With the grandmothers of the past
Foraging, healing, resolute
We demand their voices be unearthed
Releasing a haven of spirit
That we must inherit & own

Reclaiming our sacred circle
Restoring the feminine
Let our divinity flow red

WILDLY *beautiful*

What is beauty?

Is it the sprinkle of freckles across your face
Or smooth chestnut skin that glows
The twinkle in your eye, the curve of full lashes
Big teeth, glasses, piercings, or tattoos
Lipstick, high heels, braces, or jewellery
Your long flowing locks, curled into soft waves
Your shaved head—exposed, bare & gorgeously vulnerable

It is the hijab you wear proudly
The short skirts & crop tops
A jersey, coveralls, or hard hat
The tightly fit dress of sequins
Sweats & a worn, cosy t-shirt
A uniform, costume, or brand name
Do I need to be covered or bare to be beautiful?

What if I enjoy singing, fencing & painting my nails
& I scream when my temper flares
& I stick my tongue out when I feel like it
What if I love with all my being
With a passion that burns from within
What if I like to get dirty
Because I work hard & love jumping in puddles?

Is there beauty in my crooked smile
In the scars upon my body
Do you see a disability
Or the strength of my resilience
Even princesses can be warriors
Disease, lies, those that want to keep me small
Don't stand a chance

Friend, sister, mother
Leader, fighter, game changer
We will teach each other to
Braid hair, ride a horse, spike a ball
Climb a tree, catch a fish, write a speech
To have curiosity, to be fearless, to stand tall
Create more love, poetry & justice

To be unapologetically ourselves
For all these things & more
Are wildly beautiful

WILDLY *beautiful* too

What does it mean to be beautiful?
Is that what we are to strive for? Beauty?
A defined construct of size, demeanour & flair
Do you earn it with silence & conformity
Or is it evident in my loud, outspoken voice?
Is it seeking uniform ideals
Lovers, but not too many
Success, marriage, kids?
Is my beauty confirmed with a beau by my side
Someone that craves me
Prized for my curves, smile, breasts?
Am I beautiful if I go after what I want
Following my lust & finding my pleasure
Or is it in my modesty, my willingness to submit?

And once I've met these imposed ideals
Am I still beautiful?
Is it there in the ache of my feet & pounding of my head
After the arduous cycle of duty?
Can you see it as I swell with a developing soul?
Is it in my saggy breasts
After having nourished fresh babes?
What about in my loose flesh
Scarred with the reminder of creating life?
Am I beautiful if I remain unaltered
Never striving for more
Content with my nice, happy life?

Or does beauty grow like the blossoming of a flower
Sparking the anticipation of more
Gently unfurling boundless potential
Developing, expanding
Believing, embracing & freeing?
It is in my decisions
No more seeking answers from others
Rather, choosing to discover it within
Honouring my true self
Becoming a mother IF I CHOOSE to be one
Working, because I am a Bitch Boss
Staying single, strong, independent
Showing the world that I can, I will
Making them realize there IS a choice
So choose to be beautiful
Just as you are
For YOU alone can decide to be
Wildly Beautiful too

OUR *love* is

butterfly kisses ● cold toes on warm legs ● you playing
with my hair ● back scratches ● holding hands ● playing
games ● sticky notes ● frustrating ● postcards from places
we have been together ● complicated ● love letters ● trust
● surprising one another ● thoughtful ● patient ● kind
● listening ● Netflix & chill ● homemade ● laughter
● ((HUGS)) ● Scrabble ● falling asleep in each other's
arms ● showering together ● getting up with the kids ●
coming along for the ride ● phone calls to say goodnight ●
hanging out ● silent ● walks on the ridge ● cutting your
hair ● goodnight kisses ● unconditional ● you emptying
the compost ● weekends away ● keeper emails ● tough
conversations ● warming up the car ● supportive ●
keeping the lights on ● a road trip partner ● family game
night ● couch naps ● passionate ● a touch on the shoulder
● a squeeze of the ass ● having a dance partner ● work ●
Manitoba ● finding each other funny more than anyone
else would ● brushing the snow off the car ● bringing me
coffee ● fun ● growing ● creating family traditions ● me
finding my favourite chocolate bar hidden in the fridge
● you buying me Captain Crunch or baguette & brie ●
staying at the table until I'm done eating ● date days ●
being held while I cry ● quiet ● making decisions ● you
buying me flowers ● doing our own thing ● alone time
● happy ● solid ● coming to read with me ● lasting ● an
adventure ● a promise ● seen in a smile ● a fairy tale ●
romantic ● April Fool's tricks ● special ● a high school
romance ● a story ● evolving ● appreciated ● chosen ●

poetic ● full of memories ● a gift ● respect ● a joint effort
● a great model for our children ● disagreeing at times ●
celebrated ● sharing values ● apparent ● home together ●
cherished ● you slowing down for me ● forever

Creating a beautiful family ❤
    One that gets to live in our very own fairy tale ❤
    A never-ending love story ❤

Autumn Recital

REFLECT & REMEMBER

RUDENEJA

The truth
g e n t l y
> F
> A
> L
> L
> I
> N
> G

Into place
Remembering what matters
Forgetting the rest
Shedding layers that
Served to protect you
Your armour no longer needed
As you step into
Yourself

RUDENEJA—Lithuanian
[ROO-den-Ay-HA] (v.) the way nature and/or the weather
begins to feel like autumn

REMEMBER

What was that?
fleeting thought
& Back

What was that?
dull ache
& Back

What was that?
hidden feeling
& Back

What was that?
soft whisper
& Back

What was that?
inviting call
& Back

What was that?
insightful twinge
& Back

What was that?
tugging heartstrings
& Back

What was that?
glowing light
& Back

What was that?
arousing soul
I Stand Firm
I KNOW what that is ...
I am Remembering
No Going Back

SEEK

There is more
To me
To life
I know this
As I know
The world
Is wide &
Expansive

I crave &
Yearn answers
It feels urgent
Like a deep hunger
Desperation spreads
Throughout my body
My thoughts
Are overtaken

But in the seeking
I am missing
Out on the
Here & now
Direction will come
When the time
Is right
I must trust

In the meantime,
I need to be
Present, awake
So I recognize
The opportunity
When it arrives
With a calling
Loud & clear

So I learn to
S L O W
Down
To trust
To wait
To listen
With a
Hopeful spirit

DESIRE

What do I desire?
I feel I Should desire
Wealth, success
A vacation home or two
Designer shoes
A fancy new car

BUT

If I drop the Should
I find a happier place
Where dreams are
Within reach
Without breaking
Myself apart

I desire open space
Where I can be free
Unapologetically myself
Basking in the stilled expanse
Appreciating the sky above
& the life thriving beneath my feet

I desire nature
To settle myself in a meadow
Of moss, grass & flowers
To lean against a proud popular
Rooted, wise & welcoming
I let my soul be replenished

I desire simplicity
Joy in a freshly laid egg
Hope in a birdsong
Finding connection
Among the plants & animals
That share the homeland

I desire community
Where people come together
To share, learn & grow
We can listen & hold space
Gathered within a circle
A place where we can be accepted

I desire motion
For my incredible body
To move freely in the world
To dance with the stars
To walk with confidence
Radiating with purpose

I desire pleasure
From a lover's touch
To the site of a rainbow
The feel of rain on my
Naked body as I dance
To my own beautiful song

I desire abundance
In life & love
In compassion & understanding
I will nurture a big, full life
Accepted with a grateful heart
May my cup runneth over

THESE EXPECTATIONS

Have been implanted in my fertile being
Throughout the many moons of my life
While I was blissfully daydreaming
Unaware & without my consent
Installed by an institutional brotherhood
To force & keep me complacent

These expectations
Have cultivated strong seeds
Rooted deep within me
Beliefs that can be found
Entangled around my heart
Imbedded in my spirit

These expectations
Are absorbed & grow into my reality
They anchor down in my subconscious
Eternally present to admonish me
Don't lose sight of your obligations
You need to ... you should ...

These expectations
Have been tended & watered
By myself & others
With an intention to ripen & flourish
Establishing pride for myself & others
I believe I can fulfil my potential

These expectations
Are sprouting into a variant
Rising with resentment & frustration
They have evolved into resistance
Demanding & persistent
I cannot escape them

These expectations
Unfold into a misguided
Comparison of veracity vs rot
I am repeatedly uprooted
My time & vitality scattered
I doubt my ability to sustain life

These expectations
Are not designed for me to thrive
They are calculated to keep me engaged
Distracted & exhausted
So I am invariably left feeling unsettled
Disoriented & severed from myself

These expectations
Are like limbs branching out
It can be hard to distinguish
Between where **I** am
& where **They** begin
As I develop over the seasons
I blossom with understanding

These expectations
Are greed & power
Planted in our world
To control & manipulate
To form a perception & judgement
That you are not enough

These expectations
Will be contested as I unearth
Remembering my own seedlings of verity
Buried deep within my bones
The truth sown on my soul
As I expand, I will strive for freedom

These expectations
Will be challenged by my battle cry
By the virtue of a collection of voices
From the strength we possess together
Grounded within our knowing
WE ARE ENOUGH

heartsong

I was born with a song in my heart
One that guides & comforts me
That leads me North
When I am wandering, questioning
The song is there
Steady & true
Patient for my openness

It is the truth of my ancestors
Their hopes & dreams
The might-have-beens
Sweet, melancholy
A natural, pure rhythm
With fear, suppression & expectation
At the root of the pulse

I am born of a lineage of Brave, Beautiful souls
Each unique in thought & feeling
Each a piece of the Whole
We are all One
Past, present, future
I honour their sacrifice
I admire their strength of spirit

They have forged a path for me
So that I may lead
My one glorious life
Their lives are acknowledged
Gratitude is extended
Now I must clear new trails
For those that come after

My ancestors *were* - so I could *be*

SANCTUARY

Allow me to paint you a picture
That can be brushed to life
With a montage of poetic sensuality
I guide you to a sanctuary that I visit daily
A haven that evokes peacefulness
Swathed in layers of comfort
Here, I experience true embodiment
I invite you to awaken your senses
To facilitate this composition in your mind

Light & Dark
From the luminous sunlight peeking through
To the shadowed silence of rest
I can lay myself bare, naked with my truth
Within these inviting, calming walls
Here I am enduringly authentic
Open, vulnerable, exposed
Revealing the stigmas I'm unable to shed
This is a safe space

Smoky & Earthy
From the offering of burnt sage
To the aura of Gaia's fragrances
Here I bathe myself in incense
Allowing the dancing tendrils
To immerse within my surroundings
Diffused to purify the air
It is a bouquet of gratitude & pleasure
From Mother Earth herself

Smooth & Sticky
From the opulence of comfy sheets
To the stickiness of satisfied desire
I allow myself to be fully seen
Those parts that are robust
Imbued with a fierce sense of worth
To my infinite rough edges
Dominated by secret shames
Eternally a part of my anatomy

Sweet & Spicy
From the honeyed lip balm
To the juicy taste of my ripe, swollen sex
Eager to be taken, devoured
I can ride or be ridden
With an unbridled passion
Coming together, pure & spent
Entwined into a single scorched soul
Melted together with a radiating heat

Life & Silence
From the music that awakens my dance
To the stillness of Earth's slumber
I welcome both into my spirit
Recognizing each day as the gift it is
I aspire to honour that blessing
The harmony found here allows me
To bliss out to my own intimate song
Inspired by my one precious life

I ask, can you visualise this original painting?
Is your appetite ravenous for the tangy taste of lust?
Are you enveloped in the tantalising aroma in the air?
Do you feel the rejuvenating energy brush across your skin?
Can you hear the invitation being called out?
The richness of these experiences is embedded
Within the physical space portrayed
As well as the temple grounded within my body
I seize the opportunity to cultivate both

One can unearth these sensations
Found nestled within this idyllic space
A sanctuary that is imperfectly perfect
It is essential for us all to have one
A place to love, cry, hope
To experience the liberty of being unbound & free
To radically love & pleasure ourselves
& if we choose to share this sacred niche
Make sure they are worthy of YOU

I find as the daylight draws its final breaths
I am called upon once again
To release the burden of expectation
To choose absolution for my soul
I am in the bosom of home
Now I lay me down to sleep
Cradled in my own sure embrace
Confident, I am enough
I drift off to my own soothing lullaby

And then, my eyes flutter open to a fresh dawn
A sweet, slow smile spreads across my face
I decide to gift myself the luxury
Of staying in my warm, snug cocoon
Cherishing my serene, dreamy sleep
I take this interlude for myself
To bask in the glory of the sunrise
Thankful for this personal refuge
What will my sanctuary offer me today?

RELEASE—

I come to the water & breathe
I rest my feet in the brisk, rushing creek
   My soles massaged by the smooth, arched rocks
   I let the melody of moving water envelope me
      A boundless babble rejoicing the journey
      This ballad saturates me
        Replenishing my parched soul
        I lounge in the Sun, basking in her warmth
I ask that my fears be washed away
Carried along in the swift current
   Absorbed in the rush of ever flowing energy
   Released with love & forgiveness
      So that others may receive what they need
      When they too, come to the water

TRUE FACE

Does anyone ever truly see you?
When you look in the mirror,
Who do you see?
Someone you love & admire?
Someone you trust & respect?
Someone who has your back?
Who do you see?

MY TRUTH

I believe in a power greater than myself
A force found with us all
Others teach a path that leads beyond
So where lies the truth?

Ancestor to ancestor
An open channel
From mother to child
It is embodied in our minds
Imprinted on our souls
It is difficult to destroy

But they try & often succeed
Taught to seek it outside ourselves
Rather than trusting the insight from within
Unknowing generations of truth
Is no meagre feat

Some would rather not question
Some don't hear, others ignore
While some fight to free themselves of this
dis-ease
If they don't, they will perish
Consumed by an illness disguised as truth
New beliefs that have settled in their bones

After generations of deception
Our ancestors' gospel was rewritten
Their stories stolen & buried
Under control, power & greed
Lost to the earth

But the homeland has been nurtured
Held lovingly by Mother
It is luxuriously plush
Thriving with certainty
For the truth will not be repressed
It is richer, truer & ready
Let us remember our fierceness
Our wild that was domesticated
Trained out of us
Only to be unleashed with tenacity
Courage, strength & heart

What do I believe in?
I believe in the power of **ME**

just ME

Why do I need to explain myself
I don't want to fit in one of your boxes

        ☒ male   ☒ other
        ☒ white   ☒ other
        ☒ straight   ☒ other
        ☒ married   ☒ other
        ☒ happy   ☒ other

                 You cannot see my light
       From within the contained space
            You want to place me in

I have not been produced with rigid, uniform sides
I am shaped with soft, yummy curves
Touch me & you will see me spark
With love or anger
It is MY choice

I am here to learn, to be ever-changing
To expand with curiosity & love
I will not stay the same
Alone in the little box you have created for me
Caged to keep me small & obedient

I am a dreamer
Fuelled by hope
My powerful imagination will create
A world with no boxes
A place where we can all safely be

☒ **ME**
& that is enough

Winter Recital

REST & RECOVER

Apricity

An intrinsic, poetic melody
A harmonious essence
That caresses the face
Of those spirited enough
To venture forth on a
Brisk winter's day

APRICITY—Latin
[a-pri-ci-ty] (n.) the warmth of the sun in winter

INHALATION

nourishing my weary soul

breathing in

the repose

of rest

&

recovery

SILENCE OF WINTER

There is beauty
To be found
Within the stillness

HEALING

An arduous & isolating pilgrimage
A practice in patience & acceptance
My entity is uprooted
Placed on an unheralded path
The life I breathed to fruition
Is now a bygone era

I've entered a dystopian world
Where I instantly feel transmuted
Confined to an unfamiliar territory
I am consumed with a foreign language
Vibrating from a dormant nook
An unknown tongue from within

My introspection is fuelled
With doubt, frustration & anger
I am disoriented, lost, broken
A darkness lurks close by
Eager to feed off my light
Will I find myself again

I am no longer in control
I did not choose this
It chose me
What is this here to teach me
What do I need from this experience
To fulfil my destiny

As I lay in emptiness
I contemplate my journey
Of which my healing is a vital piece
I aspire to attain self-compassion
& subdue the foreboding thoughts
Surrendering to the lessons offered

I am open
I am trying
I am learning
I am healing

LULLABY

Twinkle, twinkle little star
How I wonder who we are
Thoughts swirl around my head
How to calm them, it's time for bed

It's time to sleep
So let's count those sheep
One, two, three, four
Let's chase them out the door

Starlight, star bright
It's time to shut off the light
Pull up the covers & tuck in tight
& don't let those bed bugs bite

Rock-a-by-baby
All snug in your bed
Let your breath out
It's time those worries shed

Hush little darling
Close your eyes
It's time to sing you a lullaby
Now drift off into those starry skies

Now I lay me down to sleep
Restoration full & deep
Feeling renewed as I wake
I light my sage & mediate

& now ...

I rest

Bouquets of Thanks

Bryce—*my other half*—for seeing Me, choosing Me, loving Me

Chloe, Zak, Sophie & Josie—*my greatest teachers*—you made my dream come true

Molly & Dale—*mom & dad*—for showing me what unconditional love looks & feels like

Finnegan—*loyal walking companion & goldendoodle extraordinaire*—I have never experienced a love like yours before

Lindsey—*friend, illustrator, book club co-chair*—for adding your beautiful light to this book
- @lindseyhopkinsart

Sharon—*mentor & friend*—for inviting me to the poetry of yoga class that opened me up

Friends—*near & far*—for the endless support & laughter—you polish my Shine

Tellwell—*self publishing gurus*—for helping me make this dream a reality

Glennon, Abby & Sister—*podsquad guides*—you will see inspiration from your show sprinkled throughout my work—"I am a goddamn cheetah"

My Ancestors for all the steps you did & didn't take; I honour you

Mother Earth for the lessons & beauty—may we do/be better

The ridge for my inspiration & wellness

These poems were written on, & inspired by, Treaty 7 lands.

In the spirit of reconciliation, I acknowledge that I live, work & play on the traditional territories of the Blackfoot Confederacy (Siksika, Kainai, Piikani), the Tsuut'ina, the Îyâxe Nakoda Nations, the Métis Nation (Region 3), & all people who make their homes in the Treaty 7 region of Southern Alberta.

Finale

TRIBUTE

GRUMPY GRAMPS

Mornings weren't his thing,
Tired eyes & grunts before coffee
Homemade toast with THICK butter
He sits at the table with his bare, hairy chest
Please don't belch, Grandpa

A grumpy demeanour was put on
His eyes & face said it all
But then there was the angel
Singing with heart & soul
Touching those around him

He sang & preached
Taught & coached
Mentored & challenged
Saved & restored faith
He was giving of himself

You always knew where he was
Just follow the gentle hum/whistle
For it could always be heard
Or just wait for meal time
Hark to the Chimes

Fond memories from the past
Riding along in his homemade wagon
Was it a wagon?
His electric bike buzzing to life
Trips to the cemetery were expected

Summer time we would visit
Swimming lessons & cable TV
Loved those game shows
Grandpa watching from his chair
Commercials were silenced

Hot, humid days outside
Hiding in the garage watching
Nature's light show in the sky
While the lawn displayed perfection
Lush, green & precise

Fresh garden veggies
Ripe for the picking
Sweet & juicy in the mouth
Green onions straight from the garden
Pass the salt, please

Eating, driving, family, community
All things that made him smile
He was proud of those he loved
He always had hugs & kisses
For all of his angels

I am but one

in honour of Stewart John Anderson
1928–2017

WILD BILL

It's a blessing to grow up
With grandparents close by
Walking distance
Made visits frequent
At home in that beautiful
Cold, old house
There would always be
Snick snacks
A fire in the winter
Religiously tended by Grandpa
There was shared laughter
While I read from
The *Reader's Digest*
Grandpa loved a
Good joke!
Crokinole, rummoli
Rummy, sequence, wizard
He played cards
Til the end
Along with his
Puzzles & daily
Apartment walks
Grandpa kept his
Body & mind active

The farm was always home
I remember lunch
In the fields
A thermos full
Of sweet lemonade
Grandpa taking a
Break with us
When he was at work
We explored the land
Finding morels
At the right time of year
Catching tadpoles
In the creek out front
An old creaky outhouse
To do our business
Picking strawberries & raspberries
I wasn't much help I'm sure
Finding a shady spot
To sit on an overturned pail
Later he built
A treehouse &
Cleared walking trails
Through the trees
It's a peaceful place to be

His attire was consistent
Slacks & long sleeve
Button up, plaid shirt
He was always
Put together
I don't think
I ever saw
His arms
& rarely his legs
Which were blindingly white
A hat upon his head
& later
Sunglasses always
In place
Grandpa aged gracefully
He seemed to always
Look the same
A big smile in place
A body that shook
With laughter
He liked his coffee
Cookies & sweets
He was catered to
Everything done just right

Grandpa was a
Natural storyteller
I loved hearing
About the olden days
His memory was sharp
Recalling specific years
Just like that
If you brought up politics
Be prepared
To stay awhile
& watch
Grandma roll her eyes
& then glare his way
He could predict the weather
Do mental math
& at age 93
He practically aced
His cognitive test
He definitely did
Something right
To stay strong
In mind & body
We have much
To learn from him

What would Grandpa
Say is the secret
To a long & full life?
Keep family close
Keep laughing
Tell those jokes
The raunchier the better
Grow your own food
So you can eat healthy
Buy only what you need
Be grateful
For what you have
Don't take
Things for granted
Keep moving
Shuffling back & forth
To serve the daily
Snick snack
Is one of the best ways
To do so
Keep your mouth shut
Stay positive
Love those around you
SMILE:)

Thank you, Grandpa
For showing us
What a loving
Man, husband,
Father & grandpa
Should look like
We are all better
For having known you
Your legacy will
Continue on through
The generations
You have given us
A strong foundation
A place to thrive from
You've shown us what hard work
& dedication looks like
It brings me such joy
To know that you are in the
Arms of your parents
Speaking German again
I hope you are howling
At the moon with your brother
With thanks & love
Bless you, Grandpa

in honour of William Harold Pohl
1929–2023

home

A dwelling of comfort
Security, lifelong teachings
A nest of sustenance & guidance
A place that accepts You
Embraces you through hardships
Surrounds you with laughter
Bathes you in warmth & love

Your first ever home was Me
You started as a sparkle in my eye
Then my body welcomed you
Your passage an expression of love
A pure, authentic miracle
Of thousands, you are One
We chose each other

You pronounced me home
Bedding yourself down
Settling into the warmth of my womb
My elation was palpable
Feeling your butterfly kisses
From deep within my walls
Your dancing made me glow

I swaddled you with protection & nourishment
Furnished you a room all your own
A warm sea to grow & glide through
A haven to explore
My heartbeat a steady drum
My voice a soothing song
Cherished time, just the two of us

A birthing of both mother & child
A further generation
Your initial home

My first true love

*for Chloe, Zak, Sophie & Josie, in honour of Mother's Day

YOU *loved* me

You loved me before I loved myself

How it is that someone can
Look at you & see what
No one else can
To feel a connection & desire
To choose acceptance & love
Faults, scars & all
To let the annoyances slide
To support every dream & choice
To not question me
Even when I question myself

I try to see myself the way you do
With unconditional love
Pure, simple, sweet
When I do this
I come closer to seeing my light
That which makes me special
Your love makes me strong
It makes me believe in miracles
While I can doubt myself
I never doubt your love

& that is **enough**

for Bryce, in celebration of our 20th wedding anniversary

Should I ...

Skinny dip ● pierce my nose ● climb a mountain ● change careers ● dye my hair ● love my wrinkles ● embrace my hairy legs ● stop wearing makeup ● say no without explanation ● shave my head ● have 4 kids in 4 years ● move to a new town ● write a poem ● trust myself ● wear pjs grocery shopping ● speak my truth ● have that tough conversation ● dance like nobody's watching ● lay in the sun all afternoon ● leave a tip ● have another couch nap ● leave early ● question everything ● take care of myself ● go on medication for my depression & anxiety ● talk openly about my mental health ● know my worth ● ask for what I want ● celebrate my awesomeness ● pee in the pool (sometimes it just happens) ● use baby wipes on my sweet ass ● see a therapist ● forgive myself ● pick my nose ● believe everything is going to be OK ● seek understanding ● pay for the person behind me ● keep the $50 bill I found on the ground ● accept help ● bake my own bread ● wash my own windows ● dance in the rain ● look up at the stars ● be curious ● swear ● apologize ● listen ● take a bath ● accept ● marry my first love ● follow my heart ● learn from my experiences ● express gratitude ● go on dates with my kids ● say please & thank you ● acknowledge good customer service ● travel ● camp in a '73 VW camper van ● name my vehicles (the camper van is Ernie) ● talk to my plants ● love myself ● try new things ... or not ● don't sweat the small stuff ● love my cottage cheese legs & ass ● shine unapologetically ● visit museums ● ignore advice ● participate in a poetry night ● be a stay-at-home mom until all my kids are in school ● live on a budget ● buy that book • not give out gift bags at birthday parties • shop at thrift stores • treat myself to Starbucks • let my kids figure out their own shit • wait to get home to poop • crave a simple life • learn my family history • phone my mom & dad • buy that lot with a view & build a house • be angry that necessary feminine products are pricey • go to sleep before my kids get home • admit my beliefs are different • bring you homemade soup when you're feeling down • be happy to get away from my kids • go on family road trips • save for a family vacation to Hawaii • hide a Barbie head around the house • go braless • learn from history • eat sugar • smell the flowers • be open to new ideas • be sensual • honour my ancestors • be proud of my age • hug students at school • hug anyone for that matter • make my kids pay for their own phones & plans • tell you there's something in your teeth • eat a lot of cookie dough • take my first flight overseas by myself as an 18 year old • shit in the bush • continue to fight the fight • pee on the side of the road • not shower ... again • read another chapter • strike up a conversation with a stranger • tell them their smile lights up their face • pop that zit • crack my knuckles • paint that wall purple • buy a second-hand '70s chesterfield (see what I did there?) • grow a full bush • participate in drumming circles • enjoy a second helping • hoard that box of Captain Crunch (I'm not sharing) • cry in front of my kids • masturbate • choose colour • express myself • admit that I don't know • be patient • clean out my closet • ignore the mess • Netflix & chill • visit the library • laugh loudly • binge watch *Working Moms* • take that painting class • donate those pants that no longer fit • learn from others • express appreciation • lose my shit when the kitchen is dirty 10 minutes after I finish cleaning it • say I love you • vote • get another houseplant • try to hide my latest thrift shop find • break rules that are stupid • respect tradition • add my own personal flair • name my houseplants & trees • house 17 family members in my home over the Christmas holidays • drive to Texas • rave about finding the perfect pen • add something I already did to my TO DO list just to have the satisfaction of crossing it off • respect elders (unless they give me reason not to) • stick up for my friends • give myself a gold star (literally) • leave uncomfortable situations • try • get out for a walk • keep my mouth shut • trust my instincts • roll my eyes • ask the same question again as I admit I didn't listen the first time • plant a garden • form my own opinions • write a Wellness proposal & present it to my boss • implement a Wellness program at our school • have dessert • walk away from drama • stand in awe of crocuses EVERY.SINGLE.YEAR (no matter what my kids say) • see the goodness • hope • remember • wear the shirt my kids made me • spread sticky note love • perform random acts of kindness • write my grandma a letter • double flush • show up fully • follow *We Can Do Hard Things* • listen to another episode • write love letters • go to a nude beach (so freeing) • show my weaknesses • walk with my head held high • eat whatever I want, whenever I want • get a dog • look at old pictures • change the world • admit when I'm wrong (which is rare) • want a warm car to get into when it is cold outside • work on expanding myself • challenge accepted norms • go sliding with my kids • stop wearing uncomfortable clothes • feel all the feels • buy myself flowers • believe in myself • sing • trust my kids •

miss my hometown ● know that life comes with struggles ● be able to handle anything ● stay in bed ● go barefoot ● day dream ● curl up with a good book ● admit I don't know your name ● accept the good with the bad ● fight back ● let that insult roll off my back ● stretch ● let the sunshine in ● turn up the music ● seek beauty (it's EVERYWHERE) ● get angry ● be lazy ● add more pepper ● ask the hard question ● make donations ● become more & more hippie-like the older I get ● ask for no olives ● stop dyeing my hair ● see their side ● add that poem that doesn't really fit the theme ● share myself ● publish a book of my poetry

While I'm not typically a **SHOULD** girl …

the answer I get back is clear …

you sure-shittin' should!!

... & I did ♥

THIS IS NOT THE END,

... merely a new beginning

About the Author

Tenneil is a prairie girl at heart, born & raised in Manitoba. She is now happily settled in the foothills near the Canadian Rocky Mountains. Tenneil is home among family & friends, animals & nature, books & bread. She can be found walking her dog on the ridge behind her home, playing cards with her family, reading a book, cuddling on the couch, or dancing until her feet hurt.

Tenneil discovered her love of writing poetry during the isolation of COVID. She was encouraged to try writing after attending an online Poetry of Yoga class. The creative result was her first poem, entitled BREAKING THROUGH, which can be found in this book.

@goatsbeardphotographyco